Aquilina (or, The Confession Of Hatifari Maforimbo)

A novella by Masimba Musodza

Translated out of the original ChiShona text by the author. With new
material not found in the original

2nd edition published in Great Britain in 2024 by:
Carnelian Heart Publishing Ltd
Suite A
82 James Carter Road
Mildenhall
Suffolk
IP28 7DE
UK
www.carnelianheartpublishing.co.uk

Publishing History:
First published in ChiShona as *Aquilina, kana kuti Reuriro yaHatifari Maforimbo*, Amazon Kindle, 2011.
Translated into English by the author, with additional material.
First published in English as *Aquilina (or, the Confession of Hatifari Maforimbo)* in print and e-book edition, by Belontos Books, 2019.

Copyright ©Masimba Musodza 2024

Paperback ISBN   978-1-914287-85-5
eBook ISBN   978-1-914287-86-2

Editors:
Panashe Nyagwambo & Samantha Rumbidzai Vazhure

Cover design: Masimba Musodza

Typeset by Carnelian Heart Publishing Ltd
Layout and formatting by DanTs Media

AUTHOR'S FOREWORD

This story belongs to the literary genre known as *Psychological Horror* in English [although I would also place it in the ghost, weird fiction and slipstream categories]. We have not yet come up with a name for this genre as it is still new to literature in ChiShona. It also builds on a popular trope of Zimbabwean urban mythology. Not wishing to give too much away, I will assume the reader is old enough to remember Peggy.

I first published this novella in 2011, feeling emboldened by the reception given to *MunaHacha Maive Nei?* by both readers and critics of literary ChiShona alike. In publishing *MunaHacha Maive Nei?* using modern methods, I felt vindicated against those who still hold that ChiShona as a language has no relevance to our age of mobile phones and the Internet. However, I could not have accomplished this without the support of the people who went out to buy the book and told others about it. Please, keep that support coming, I am deeply grateful!

Unfortunately, Amazon Kindle does not support literature in ChiShona. Today, nearly a decade and a half since I first published Aquilina, Kindle supports only two African languages; KiSwahili and Afrikaans. So, that is how the story of Aquilina fell into obscurity.

Despite this drawback, I have managed to establish a career as a storyteller. So, I have gone back to my old files to bring back stories that people have enquired about.

Sometimes, it occurs to a writer to link characters and settings across different books. I have established a reputation as a writer of detective fiction, while others are more familiar with my science fiction and horror stories, but I like to remind readers that I am the same author. In this novella, you will encounter Sgt Sambiri, known to those who have read my *Dread Eye Detective Agency* stories in English. When this story starts, the Chisango siblings were not detectives yet. They would have been still at school. In the story's conclusion, a reference to them is made. We also encounter the police detective Nyasha Zulu, who appears in the horror novel, *Herbert Wants To Come Home*.

This novella follows the literary style known as the epistolary novel in English. This style entails writing the story in the form of correspondence, diary entries, newspaper articles or other documents, such that a reader might think they are reading a factual narration rather than a work of fiction. It also helps the writer move between points of view, or change the main character. I realise that this literary style is not widely used by writers in ChiShona, so I can only hope it will be well received.

Masimba Musodza, Middlesbrough

She said and she swore, that she never would deceive me,
but the devil take the women, for they never can be easy.

- **Whiskey In The Jar**, Irish folk song.

I am quite sure she felt no pain.
As a shut bud that holds a bee,
I warily opened her eyelids: again
Laughed the blue eyes without a stain,
And I untightened next the tress
About her neck; her cheek once more
Blushed bright beneath my burning kiss:
I propped her head up as before,
Only this time my shoulder bore
Her head, which droops upon it still:
The smiling rosy little head,
So glad it has its utmost will

- **Robert Browning**, *Porphyria's Lover*

PROLOGUE

Z. R.P. Tswakata Station
P.O. Box 73
Tswakata

14 September, 1997

My dear Onesimus

Are you well, *Dziva*[1]? As for us, we are fine. Amai[2] Cindy says
to ask Amai Noma what her answer is about 'the thing.'
Personally, I resent being used as a messenger boy by our
wives. They saw each other just the other day, why didn't they
finalise on whatever it is Amai Cindy is on about? And, what
is it really that can only be referred to as 'the thing'? This is
like a hunter asking his neighbour if he can borrow a big
knife; it's inviting questions, yet not wanting to divulge
anything right away. One of these days, you will hear that I
have detained her in the interrogation room here at
Tswakata!
Never mind all that, bro, let's delve into our own 'the thing'—
the thing we were talking about the day before yesterday,
before the cellular network turned once again into a
"notwork"! This case continues to trouble me, even though,
as police, we cannot proceed with it any further. As I reflect
on it, I think it is actually a stroke of good fortune that we
could not continue to discuss it on the phone that night,
because I don't think I would have been able to furnish you
with all the information we have on it now.

---

1 Praise name for the fish totem clan.
2 "Mother of Cindy." Adults are usually referred to or addressed
by their children's names in Zimbabwean society

So, I have sent you with this letter a copy of a signed testimony written by a young man named Hatifari Maforimbo, who came to the station and told us that he had just murdered a lady named Aquilina. He claims that they have been living together for four months, but they were not married.

I am asking you to read Maforimbo's statement and then my report. I tell you, those who have already died did not see anything!

Thanking you, I remain

L. Kweche

P.S. If you saw the W.P.C. who was transferred yesterday from Macheke, you would wonder why God created us too early, and why he put in our imprudent heads the notion that we should abandon bachelorhood so quickly! And, you'd also want a word with whoever said female officers should wear trousers! They say she has a man, but he is stationed in Zvishavane, so she may be seeking what is now called an "alternative source of energy"!! In this office, all men are at full mast all day, like boys at a boarding school who have had their porridge laced with *vhuka-vhuka*! At least I get to work off my desires on Mai Cindy when I go home after work! True, she is nowhere near the *dzambarafuta* I married, but my wife doesn't wear tight slacks in a predominantly male environment. Only I get to see her special gifts. Now, this W.P.C. spends the shift bent over the counter, talking to members of the public who come in to report a crime or something. When she is writing, all of "this" shakes and jiggles! My desk is directly behind her, so I have a front row seat at this titillating feast. It is a sight one cannot get used to, my friend! I don't know if we can beat temptation, please pray for us!

CHAPTER 1

The Confession of Hatifari Maforimbo

ZIMBABWE REPUBLIC POLICE - MASHONALAND EAST COMMAND

STATEMENT FORM

GIVEN NAME: *Hatifari* **FAMILY NAME**: *Maforimbo*
PREVIOUS NAME (IF DIFFERENT FROM ABOVE): *N/A*
DATE OF BIRTH: *11/04/73*
NATIONAL IDENTITY NUMBER: *63-47640901-W-21*
ADDRESS: *St Damian's Secondary School, PO Box 17, Tswakata Township*
DISTRICT: *Goromonzi*
TELEPHONE NUMBER: 011 730 544

ABOUT THE STATEMENT:

Place where written: TSAKWATA POLICE STATION
Date: 19 August 1997
Time: 11:37

STATEMENT

First, I would like to thank you, sir, for allowing me this chance to narrate fully the events of my life which have led to me murdering Aquilina. This shows that even you acknowledge it is not an everyday occurrence for a human being, no matter how enraged they might be, to murder another. But, I don't know where to begin. I see my whole life as having marched inexorably to this stage, where I am found committing such a heinous crime.

My name is Hatifari Maforimbo. I have been told that I was so named because one of my uncles, my mother's youngest brother, died in a car accident the day I was born. So, my maternal grandmother said we do not rejoice at the news of the birth as we are mourning our own child.

I am the eldest son, but the second child born to my mother. After me, my mother had four more children, each with its own father. My parents separated when I was in Grade 2. My sister, Matilda, was in Grade 4.

Sir, like me, you are a man. In your line of work, you may have seen many things, but I don't think you would look at the reason my parents separated lightly, leading as it did to my humiliation and degradation by society. So, you must understand that it is not easy for me to dwell on such things, even at this time when I narrate them on this paper. But I have committed myself to confessing fully, and this is what I must do now.

Father was a teacher at a rural school, so he spent most of the month there, including two weekends. So, we, his children, mostly saw him during the holidays. We lived in Mufakose, a suburb of Harare, in an area where the houses had only one bedroom. When Father was away at work, we slept with Mother on their bed. But, when Father was around, Mati and I slept on the floor in the sitting room. However, there were days when I woke up and found Mati and I had slept on the floor in the sitting room, even though Father had not come home from work, and I would remember clearly that we had gone to sleep on the bed the night before. On one such day, I woke up and ran to the bedroom. There was indeed a figure lying next to Mother, but she angrily ordered me out of the room, and shut the door. On another, I asked her why we had found ourselves on the floor in the living room, having gone to sleep in the bedroom. I was scolded and told I was too clever for my own good, and this would get me into trouble soon. I asked Mati what the meaning of this strange phenomenon was. She did not scold me, but I think she knew exactly what was going on.

One day, I asked Father why he didn't bring us sweets the last time he had come home. He said he had not come home the previous weekend, and there was this thoughtful expression on his face.

On another night, I woke up from a bad dream, which began to fade from my memory immediately, and found Mati and I in the living room again. I got up and ran to the bedroom. The door was ajar, but that is not what made me pause, all senses alert. The curtains were drawn, but there was a full moon outside, and the entire house was bathed in grey.

There were two people on the bed. On top of Mother, such that you could only see her legs splayed out from under him and meeting over his huge back in a lock hold, was this giant with a bald head out of which sweat poured like water out of a loofah being squeezed after use. His buttocks rose and slammed back down so furiously, accompanied by the sounds of wet, bare flesh slapping against flesh, my first interpretation of what I was seeing was that my mother was the victim of a violent attack by an intruder. Then I realised she was holding onto him, her arms around his neck, and she was sucking her breath through clenched teeth. The whole room was filled with a strange smell, a combination of tobacco, perfume, sweat and other things I could not identify.

After taking all this in, I returned to the living room and lay beside Mati. But I could not sleep. I heard them, I smelled them, long through that night. I did not understand what I had witnessed, but I knew that it was something bad, something that no one my age was meant to see. Something that Mati, with a knowing grin, said fathers and mothers did at night, but would not elaborate. So, all I knew about what I had seen was that it was bad. It was… shameful. I began to sob, overcome with shame. And that is how I drifted off to sleep eventually.

Perhaps it was a coping mechanism, but up until this day that I sit here writing this, I had erased that shocking sight of my mother engaging in adultery from my mind, just as one might erase a song from a cassette or a computer's memory. It doesn't mean that the song is no longer there, only that your device can no longer pick it up or play it again. I learnt later in life from experts on mental health that this ability to lock away bad memories is a very human one, and it enables us to move on from really traumatic experiences. I have heard of people who regain consciousness in hospital and have no idea how they got there.

But this was only one of many nights that I was to try to erase from memory. When I look back, I think this terrible night was when I really became aware of the behaviour of the women in my life, when feelings of anger towards them, of feeling betrayed and let down by them, of hating them began to germinate. I say this feeling extended to all the women in my life because I was sure that Mati knew exactly what was happening and approved of it.

One morning, I heard the footsteps of someone leaving the bedroom, and I covered my head with the blankets. The person trod right next to my face, and I felt the end of his shoelace flick against my nose before he stepped over us. I heard the door to the outside open and close before the footsteps retreated and were gone from my hearing range. My mother came out of the bedroom and locked the outside door, then went back to bed.

If Mati had seen this visitor of ours, as I am almost sure she did, she did not say or indicate so. So, I was alone with my turmoil, my anger and shame. I badly wanted to talk to someone about it, but I did not know the words with which to say what I had seen or how I felt about it. All I could do was cry whenever I was alone.

One day, Father came home during the middle of the school week and beat up Mother. Neighbours gathered to watch this "free movie", as they call such outbreaks of domestic violence in townships like Mufakose. No one lifted a finger to rescue Mother, as is usually the case in such situations. In fact, the crowd were cheering Father on, urging him to really beat her up. By the time us children had returned, the violence had stopped. We found Mother with her face swollen, relatives assembled and a family court in session. Us children spent the night at a neighbour's, the Mpofu family. The following day, Mother, Mati and I packed our bags and went to live with our maternal grandparents in Highfield.

On the day we moved in, another family court was held in Highfield, this time by our mother's relatives. Uncle Tau, one of Mother's brothers, wanted to beat her up again. Grandmother managed to restrain him and told him off. Mother, Mati and all the other females present screamed, but I found myself wanting to urge him on. Even in my youthful innocence, and with no one having explained to me what was happening, I knew that Mother had done something really bad, and it seemed fitting that she be punished. I actually wanted to mete out the punishment personally. Years later, as an adult, I came across an English song with the lyric, "*Punish Mummy for being such a whore!*" This line resonated with what was in my heart as I watched Mother try to hide behind Grandmother from Uncle Tau's blows.

I never saw Father again. When we were older, Mati tried to resume contact, but he refused to have anything more to do with us, saying that he was not even sure we were really his children. With what I saw of Mother's character and behaviour, even I had doubts that he was our father.

Mother was shamelessly promiscuous. It was said that there wasn't a man she said no to, even a relative. There is a brother of Grandmother she is reputed to have messed about with, which frosted relations between Grandmother and her brother's wife. However, reflecting on it now, I am more of the view that this uncle groomed my mother and used her when she was a child, and no one stood up to him or sought justice from the courts. This view is informed by what I read later in life about mental health issues.

On the other hand, Grandfather, Mother's father, said his daughter's behaviour was caused by a spirit that had wandered across the clan and finally settled on Mother, or that it had been sent to attach itself to her by those who knew how to do such things. There was a great-aunt who had travelled to Johannesburg and lost touch; it was there it was believed she had met an Indian worker of the dark arts, who had taught her how to evoke a prostitute's spirit, and she had died without leaving issue. Many prophets and witch doctors said this great-aunt had now attached herself to her grand-niece. Moreover, the relative who had sent this spirit to Mother, and therefore knew the necessary incantation and propitiation to bind or loosen it, did not wish to be involved, claiming that as she had now committed herself to Christianity, she did not remember the rubric to summon or expel this spirit. This spirit could allegedly bring a lot of money through prostitution; all it required in return was that the whole clan hold feasts in its honour. Grandfather refused. Perhaps his other kinsmen knew how to fortify their daughters against this spirit, for it was only Mother who manifested its presence in her life.

Grandfather and Grandmother, and some of the other relatives, tried to protect us children from being exposed to Mother's shameful lifestyle. Uncle Tau would take us, Mati and I, to spend weekends or holidays at his house in the suburbs on the other side of Samora Machel Avenue. However, Aunt Mai Berita, his wife, did not like us visiting. She was cruel, and reviled us before our cousins, until they too began to ill-treat us. One day, she beat Mati so badly, my sister broke her arm and had to be taken to hospital. That was the end of our visits to Uncle Tau. Our other maternal uncle, Amos, was the pastor of a church, one of these new ones that do the Holy Spirit thing, so he regarded Mother, his own sister, as so impure that it was not right for him as a Man of God to have anything to do with her. Mother was the only sinner, but Uncle Amos spurned us children too.

Then Grandfather died. I was in Grade 7. I was now old enough to know what it meant when Mother painted her face, put on strong perfume and tight-fitting fashionable outfits and spent many days away from home, returning with clothes, food and toys for us. Sometimes she was sad when she returned and wept for days like someone bereaved. When Grandfather died, Mother began to bring her male friends home. At first, these friends would wait at the gate and send one of us to call her. However, they soon began to relax in the lounge too. Eventually, they became brazen enough to leave the rest of the family watching TV while they went off with Mother to the shack she had built at the back of the main house. Sometimes, we would meet them the next morning as we got ready for school.

Uncle Tau came round one weekend, and brother and sister had an exchange of words, but Mother was no longer open to advice on how to live her life. Grandmother even stood up for her, saying she did not appreciate people coming over to distress her daughter, especially as said people did nothing to help her even though they could see that she was struggling to raise two children. Uncle Tau said he had washed his hands off the matter and left. All in all, Mother had nine children, but the youngest was born with the disease that now afflicted her and died in infancy. Yet, with all those children, we never saw anyone presented as the father to any of them.

I don't know who paid the fees, but I went to a mission boarding school for my secondary education, like a typical middle-class child. Obviously, the desire in sending me to such a school was so that I could have a better future – even prostitutes dream of a better future for their children. However, sending the son of a woman notorious across

Harare to be with boys from more respectable homes only exposed me to shame before my peers and highlighted how different I was from them. They would frequently start conversations with "My old man says..." Or "You really look like your father, I knew right away the moment he stepped out of the car who he had come to see at this school!"

This school was located in Masvingo, so I did not expect to meet anyone who knew me or my family. However, that very first night, the bigger boys came into our dormitory to haze us. I was asked where I came from. When I told them I was a Fio[1] lad, one of the bigger boys asked me if I, by any chance, knew Maggie. This Maggie was the sister of a corporate manager called Taurai and had another brother who was the pastor of a certain church. When I said that the Maggie he referred to was my mother, the boys burst into raucous laughter. They did not bully us after that. As they left, I overheard one of them say, "When your mother finds out that the son of your father's whore is at the same school as you, she will probably have it closed down!"

One of the other boys said, "Well, don't tell her, then. You should be thrilled to have your little brother at hand." The boys burst into another round of laughter.

The other boys in the dormitory looked at me inquiringly, but I had nothing to say. I just lay on my bed, the tears streaming. What could I say to them of that shame that I lived with?

It took a full month for me to come to terms with the fact that knowledge of my mother's waywardness was widespread at the school. I was subject to knowing looks, even from the teaching staff. I overheard snide remarks that

---

[1] Nickname for Highfield, a suburb of Harare

were clearly directed at me, even if the speaker was looking in a different direction.

There was one senior boy, Chikwanda, who had rehashed that old song by Zexie Manatsa, with the refrain, "We are united here in Zimbabwe[1]." He would come into our dorm and sing his version, "Me and my whore are embracing here in this blanket" and we had to respond with, "We are embracing, we are embracing."

One time, he really got carried away and, with his eyes on me, sang, "Me and my Maggie, we are embracing in this blanket!" Immediately, he was on his back on the floor, with me on top of him. I raised my hand, and the spoon I held flashed as it caught the overhead light, before I plunged it into his eye. Chikwanda was rushed to hospital, but the damage was done. I was expelled and finished the rest of my secondary education at one of the township schools in Highfield.

This was the first and last time I physically fought with anyone over Mother's behaviour. But there were many women who came round to our home to make scenes over their husbands. There was one occasion where this man lived with us for a whole year; it was said he had abandoned his wife and children to live with Mother. Eventually, his relatives intervened and came to remove him by force and he resisted fiercely. His relatives were convinced he had been given a love potion by Mother.

I reached an age where I began to take an interest in the opposite sex and fell in love with a really beautiful girl called Emilia. When I told her how I felt, she did not even say she

---

[1] That is the intended meaning of the lyrics, but "takabatana muno muZimbabwe can mean, "we are holding each other here in Zimbabwe" without changing the words.

needed time to think about getting into a relationship, as is usually the case with many girls. That is how I got my first girlfriend. She was in the first form, I was in the fourth. Girls of my age frightened me because they seemed to be far more advanced in their knowledge of what went on between a man and a woman, but I saw Emilia as young and naive. She had never even been to central Harare. This one time, I wanted to take her to town to watch a movie at the cinema, but we needed to think of a plan to get her parents to agree to let her leave the house. We decided to wait for when she would be sent on an errand that took her to or through the city centre. Once, I stole a kiss square on the lips, but I was afraid to even touch her!

However, barely a full month into the relationship, Emilia was caught in *flagrante delicto* at a seedy hotel in Norton with a businessman who owns a lot of shops at the Machipisa shopping area. The story was aired in the papers. The wife of the businessman and her friends beat up Emilia thoroughly, finishing by forcing a Coke bottle between her legs. I think these women are still serving their prison sentence, and as for Emilia, she left Harare for good.

Following this event, Mother became very ill. She never regained her health after giving birth to Cruise, her youngest. Cruise lived only for a few months before he contracted pneumonia and left us. It fell on me to nurse her. Mati was now working in town and did not always come back home from her job, saying she had slept at a friend's in order to save the bus fare. Grandmother refused to help with caring for her daughter, saying she was getting her just desserts. I think Uncle Tau wanted to help, but he did not want conflict with his wife. He sent money from time to time, but I don't think Aunt Mai Berita knew about it.

I looked after Mother until her last day. That taboo against a child washing even their mother's female kin, that is only observed when a society has not felt the impact of AIDS. With these hands, I cleaned sores on parts of my mother's body that I cannot mention, and smeared them with ointment. What else could I do? I could no longer bear her screams night and day, interspersed with Grandmother shouting that she deserved it for her harlotry.

Sir, perhaps by now you are asking yourself what such a long essay, which exposes my parent like this, has to do with my murder of Aquilina? Please, I beg your indulgence, I need to unburden my heart. I am not seeking your pity at all. But I want whoever reads this to know the journey of a man who ends up killing another human being.

During my mother's long illness, I had time to reflect on my hatred for her. At her life's end, the only legacy I could see she had bequeathed to me was shame, anger, and a low opinion of myself, both from myself and the people around me. I was truly that thing that everyone said I was; the son of a whore. This illness of hers, this slow death, I saw it as God finally seeing her wicked works and punishing her accordingly. So, as I watched her writhe and groan in agony, until she no longer had the strength to do even this, I gloated with the crazy delight of someone whose gods had finally risen to avenge him. The way I had gloated when Uncle Tau had tried to beat her up that day we moved back to her parents' home. The way I had gloated when I read in the paper about what had happened to Emilia, the image of her crawling in that hotel room, a bottle pushed between her legs, Mrs Lunga and her friends high-fiving each other vivid in my mind. The way I gloated whenever I read about or when I saw with my own eyes a woman being beaten or otherwise badly treated.

What I am trying to explain, sir, is that when I saw Mother suffer, while I laughed at her, this was the first manifestation of my own mental illness, which makes me hate women. Besides the random females I came across on the street and other public places, there were many women in my day-to-day life. There was my mother, who I saw as the prime cause behind all the problems I faced in life. My sister, Mati, who left me to look after Mother alone, saying she had gone to seek our father. My grandmother, who let Mother go astray, and allowed her to bring all those men home. Aunt Mai Berita, Uncle Tau's wife, who prevented her husband from looking after us at a time when we had no one else to turn to. Emilia, my first girlfriend, who had turned out to be just another whore who humiliated me before society so I became not only the son and brother of whores, but also the boyfriend of one. Everywhere I looked, all I could see were whores.

Mati had grown up to be no different. When she was in Form 2, she had to leave the boarding school she was attending after being found in the office of the father of one of her schoolmates, sitting on his lap. It became impossible for her to face this other girl at school. When she stopped coming home every evening after work, saying she had spent the night at a friend's place in the city centre, it was not long before rumours that she had been spotted loitering the Avenues district of the city centre began. The Avenues are where girls loiter at night, wearing coats with nothing underneath, which they open to passing vehicles as a way of soliciting. But I don't need to explain this to the police, you must be well acquainted with it, sir.

Although I hated loose women, I began to hang around the township's drinking places, picking up older women who came to wait outside the bars at closing time. A young chap of school going age in a township like Highfield would not have the means to even hope to entertain a girl his own age. These were the days before our bars were full of young girls; this was to come later, in the wake of the breakdown of families from the outbreak of the AIDS pandemic, which left many young girls orphaned and without anyone to offer moral guidance and material provision. So back then, all you could get in the bars were older women of my mother's age.

With all these things that I had to deal with, it might surprise you that I was academically gifted, particularly in the sciences. When I look back, if I had paid more attention to the arts, it is possible that I might have come across a well-written novel or a poem that really spoke to me and my condition and helped me understand my state of mind and lead me towards healing. But, as I came of age, I had no friends. I was a loner, an outcast among my peers. Society had labelled me the son of a whore and spurned me. When I was younger, many of the kids in my neighbourhood were forbidden from playing with me. Most of my friends during my childhood were outcasts too, the children of other wayward women. After Emilia, I never had another relationship with a woman that did not involve the exchange of money.

I went to university on a bursary, some programme to create opportunities for youth from the townships to study the sciences. Well, not having a girlfriend was not a big deal at university. Most of my peers did not even seem interested in girls, they spent much of their time on their studies. A few of them did have girlfriends, the sort that our society understands to be "good" girls, suitable for marriage, but they lived in their hometowns or villages, so these guys would join us in the seduction of the naive domestic staff who came from rural areas to work in the suburbs around the university. To be honest, I despised these country girls because I found them as immoral as their urban counterparts, even if they were lured into sexual activities and dumped cruelly.

The female students had begun to demand equality in society and were no longer satisfied with just talking or writing about it. They took to marching, waving placards, demonstrating for their right to wear trousers or short skirts without fear of anyone's disapproval or attempt to restrict what they wore. During one such demonstration, I threw a stone at one of the girls and cracked one of her eye sockets. At a disciplinary hearing, I was given the option of agreeing to being withdrawn from my studies or going to jail. I never finished my science degree.

My sister, Mati, organised for me to get a job with a company that made haircare products in Chitungwiza's Telcor industrial district. She gave me a sealed letter to present to the manager, a Mr Mavhura, whom she said she went to school with. Mr Mavhura read the letter, looked at me as if just by standing there I confirmed everything it said, and grinned before saying I could start work the next Monday.

I lasted nine months at the company. I was paid well, such that I began to buy things for myself and looked forward to acquiring my own residential stand and building my own house. Also, there was money coming in from the lodgers we had taken in, but we shared this with Uncle Tau and Uncle Amos. I thought of finishing my degree. There was a South

African university with a correspondence degree programme. That anger and shame that had haunted me like a curse had begun to abate. I still hated women, but I was sure the hatred was ebbing. I even found myself angered by a story I read in a paper about a widow whose house had been seized by her late husband's parents.

In the ninth month at my job, I got into a few arguments with a colleague, a guy named Wellington. This guy had finished his degree, and that made him think he was my superior on the job. He thought everyone at the company who did not have a university degree an idiot. One day, Wellington and I had an exchange that descended into a fist fight, and we were summoned to the manager's office. To my amazement, I got the blame and was accused of being insubordinate and not a team player. I was given the option of apologising to Wellington there and then or be immediately suspended for a month without pay. I refused to apologise and warned Mr Mavhura that if he tried to suspend me even for just an hour, I would bring the trade union into the matter. The manager then asked Wellington to step outside for a moment. When the latter had complied with this request, Mr Mavhura said to me, "Hati, as you stand there, who do you think you are? Don't get delusions about your place in the scheme of things, you hear? You are young, you don't know anything, you don't have anything! The saying goes 'If you hear a blind man say he will hit you, he knows what he is relying on', but as for you, boy, what are you relying on? You know your job, that I cannot dispute, but you haven't finished your degree, and you don't know a lot of people in the influential circles of the city. If I dismiss you from this job, do you really imagine that you will find another in this industry as easily? By the way, do you really know how you got this job when everyone else comes here brandishing a degree?"

This question hit me like a slap that leaves half your face numb, stars dancing before your eyes. I felt my bones lose their strength, my eyes wandered across the office, seeking a chair I could sink into. Yet, as devastated as I was by the question, I knew the answer to it. Perhaps Mr Mavhura did not see this, or, more likely he did but wanted to prolong my pain, for he unlocked a cabinet and obtained from it a thin file. "This could get me fired from my job or have me exposed in the newspapers, but this sort of thing is now so rampant, there is really nothing for me to be ashamed of. My boss might only just be irked that I did not invite him to dip his finger in this particular peanut-butter jar. Young man, I want you to read this letter, which your sister gave you to present to me when you came looking for work here."

Mr Mavhura tossed the sheet he had obtained from the file, and it landed on the desk. He stared at me, willing me with his eyes to pick it up. I did as he wished.

> *Geoffrey*
> *Dear, I am begging you to give my brother the job, just as we discussed over the phone. If you give him the job, you can come and sleep with me whenever you like. In this jungle, it is said that a little predator's appearance of health comes from eating others. So, I am using you so that my relative gets a job, and you get to use my thing! If you help my brother with what he needs, I will help you with what you need. Dear, don't let me down, please. You can even pass by my place this very evening. We can do it all night, if you wish.*
>
> *Matilda*

When I had finished reading, and looked up at Mr Mavhura, he did not have that smug grin that I had seen on all those men-friends of my mother. Mr Mavhura's face was actually contorted with rage, as if he was the offended party.

"There isn't an STD your sister did not give me! And, on top of those, AIDS!" Mr Mavhura said, trembling with rage. "See how emaciated I have become, young man! I don't ever want to see that sister of yours again! All the same, I had such a good time there, I even abandoned my family for a while! The first week of your job here, I was staying at her flat, and seemed to have forgotten the way home to my house in Waterfalls. I was even thinking of giving Amai Samantha her *gupuro*[1], totally dazzled by that thing, blissfully unaware that I was in fact feasting on decaying matter! I am not usually one to freely discuss with another man my sexual affair with his sister, but I want you to understand fully that, whether really sweet or rotting, it was your sister's little thing that got you this job. Don't you forget that and start assuming airs and graces around here!"

I staggered out of that office like a drunk man. What happened after that, even to this day, I have no recollection of. The next thing I knew, I was walking on an open space between different suburbs of Harare, following a path that trailed along a railway line. I doubt that I had actually walked all the way from Chitungwiza. I must have come from there by public transport, and dropped off at the industrial district after Mbare. Although I was disoriented and did not know how I had got there, there was no confusion about my purpose. I wanted to kill myself...

---

[1] Divorce token, usually a shilling which she must present to her father, uncle or her own brother.

Next thing I knew, I was in a hospital in Harare. Both my legs were in plaster. A nurse told me that I had thrown myself in front of a train, missed it and landed on the other side of the railway line. I had lain there for hours, passed out from the agony of two broken legs, until sunset, and was found by people returning home from work in the nearby factories. As is standard, I was referred to a psychiatrist, Dr Nobuhle Zwelani.

Being a woman, it was very hard for her to help me at first. Every time I saw her, I would scream that the doctor was a whore, just like all the other whores. However, after about ten months, I began to improve. Dr Zwelani explained to me that my particular mental health problem was called misogynistic fixations. In her opinion, it was perfectly understandable that I had developed such a problem. In my upbringing, I had met so many challenges for which I blamed women. My hatred for them did not mean that I was a bad person as such, but this misogyny could lead me to do something really bad, or even commit a crime. So, it was necessary that we worked together, the doctor and I, to quell this hatred that was poisoning my head. In Dr Zwelani's opinion, my issues were treatable, but it would require a sincere desire on my part.

Uncle Tau came to see me several times. Aunt Mai Berita came with him once. I think she came because she wanted to see a lunatic. I used such vulgar language on her, and she never came back. Uncle Amos came too and offered prayers. He began to doubt the power of prayer in my case and commended me to the sole care of the psychiatrist. Mati never set foot in the hospital, but two of my half-brothers, my mother's younger sons, Blessing and Justin, would visit once a week.

My treatment lasted a full two years. This brings us to the events leading to my murdering Aquilina. In the year 1996, Uncle Tau helped me to get a job as a science teacher at St Damian's Secondary, just outside the small township of Tswakata.

My sister, Mati, was married by then. She now knew the Lord and had cast aside her former life. She now earned a living as a cross-border trader, travelling to South Africa, Zambia, Botswana and Mozambique, selling different articles. With her husband, they were making good money, and she was able to pay tuition for the other children Mother had left. It seemed as if stability and prosperity had finally come into our lives. I looked forward to finishing my degree, there were now more universities established in Zimbabwe. One of these was exclusively long-distance.

Even so, I did not abandon my habit of picking up prostitutes in bars. City bars, rural bars, it only depended on where I was at the time. I actually had a budget out of my salary which was reserved for this, my pastime. The rural girls were always cheaper, but I liked my variety.

Have you ever heard of "Feja-Feja", sir? All the guys from Mbare, Mufakose, Glen View, Southerton and such areas know what it is. In Mbare, behind the Matapi hostels, you just turn up at night and say "feja-feja!" with your five dollars ready. In that dark, a hooker will take your money. She will pull down her knickers, turn round and bend over, hands leaning against the wall. And you go for it, right there! Just like that! At Kopje, the hookers are even cheaper; you can lie on a mattress for $2. The girls here in Tswakata are even cheaper than that. With just a bottle of Coke, you can get a girl. But I might be telling someone who already knows all this! I doubt that you even arrest them, because they would not afford the fine.

One Friday evening, I was on my way home from Harare. I was returning from dropping off at Mati's some fresh produce I had bought in Tswakata and some money, my contribution towards the upkeep of our half-siblings. As I reached the junction with the road into Mabvuku and Tafara, it occurred to me that the night was still young and there was time for me to detour into Mabvuku and see what was what. I turned left.

I reached the council beerhall at Chizhanje and was immediately caught up in the *museve*[1] riff blaring from inside. But it would require a few pints before one could begin to appreciate the vocal style of the lead singer, so I decided not to go in just yet. Besides, I had already found what I was looking for. I ran my eyes across the line of women on either side of the beerhall's entrance. Some hid in the shadows, not confident about parading themselves to sober clients, waiting for the establishment to close, when they would have greater chances with the drunk ones.

As I approached them, I could not help noticing a lack of the usual enthusiasm that one expects of women in that situation towards a man like me. Addressing no one in particular, I asked how much a quickie was. The women began to move away from me, as if I had fouled the air. I tried another group, but they too moved away. A man selling trotters and other treats popular with beerhall patrons

---

[1] Literally, "arrow," a popular music genre derived from Congolese and East African rhumba, so called because it is characterised by a guitar riff that maintains a single rhythm throughout. A main exponent of the genre during the time that this story is set is the now late Fanuel "System" Tazvida.

explained to me what was going on. "These days, it is quite scary around here, my brother. The girls are afraid to leave with a stranger. Last week, the body of a girl was found. It was badly decomposed, so the police are struggling to identify her or her next of kin. The police think the body is of one of these girls who walk in the night, and that she might have been killed by a client such as yourself, brother. Perhaps, they had a dispute over payment for services rendered. No one knows the truth. But some of the girls say there is one of them that they no longer see around here these days. They are saying she was new to the area and had no relatives or friends here, which is why no one reported her missing. All the same, everyone is frightened. So, all the girls you saw, they will only go with a client already known to them."

I decided to forget about picking up in Chizhanje. There were other places I could go, or I could forget about picking up altogether. However, I was a little irked that someone like me could be rejected by a mere prostitute! Who has ever heard of such a thing, that a hooker can stand near a beerhall, advertising herself, then run away from clients when they step up to her?

In a state of dudgeon, I returned to my car and headed back to Mutare Road. If there was any prostitution destined for this evening, Tswakata appeared to be the designated location. As I reached the intersection, the urge to take a leak I had been ignoring since I left Eastlea began to press the matter more vigorously. I got off the road and ran out of my car, heading for the bushes at top speed. There was adequate lighting from not just the stars and moon in the clear sky, but the towerlights of Chizhanje and the headlamps of my car, so there was no way I could have failed to spot anyone approaching, even if they were far off. So I can't explain how, one moment I was alone amidst the grass, maize fields and rocks and the next, I was looking at a girl standing about three metres from me.

Even now, I still remember exactly what she looked like and everything she was wearing. She was tall, nearly my height. Light complexioned, with relaxed hair that reminded me of that American boy band, the Jacksons, before they split up with Michael. She wore a grey T-shirt, with a corporate logo I could not quite make out to the top right and cream shorts that went down to her knees. I did not get a look at her shoes, but she had ankle-length socks. She had no make-up on, but she had the most cloying perfume that went for my senses like a narcotic. In her simple, girl-next-door attire, she was devastatingly attractive. I was blown away.

My first impression was she was a prostitute, and she had just been servicing a client here in the bushes. But, after what I had heard was going on in Chizhanje, it seemed unlikely she would allow him to leave her on her own in the bushes. Moreover, given how good the lighting was, it was undeniable that there was no one else around besides the girl and I.

It then occurred to me that she might have just come from the villages on the other side of Mutare Road and was in fact on her way to Chizhanje to engage in prostitution. There was no other plausible explanation for her presence that I could think of at the time. Yet, I had not seen her coming from the direction of Mutare Road.

"What's up, girl?" I accosted her, trying to sound brave.

"Nothing much, boy," she replied, a little stand-offish.

"Is everything okay, that you are standing in the middle of the bush like this?"

"Oh, everything is fine. Just waiting for the boys, you know."

"Well, the boys you seek are the ones you see," I said. "So, how about we go to Tswakata?"

"Tswakata?" She frowned. "Now, where is that?"

"Never mind where that is, girl," I said, grinning. "My car will take us there, let's just go."

She looked past me, at my car, "What about the money?"

I asked her how much she wanted for a whole weekend, after which I would drive her back on Sunday evening. We agreed at $60 and set off.

Along the way, she told me a little about herself. Her name was Aquilina, and she came from Chegutu. She had come to Harare to see for herself what life in a big city was like. Now, she had had enough of it, so she was delighted to have met someone who could take her to a new place. I wanted to ask her about the girl whose body had been found in Chizhanje. It occurred to me that the body had been found in that very area where I picked up Aquilina. However, Chunky Phiri's *Tamari*, a song I really liked, came on the radio and I forgot about it, the way someone who turns the page of a newspaper forgets an item he has just read. My mind turned to other matters, such as the softness of her thigh against mine.

It was midnight when we reached Tswakata. When I recall this, I find it quite puzzling, as we had left Harare at around 7pm, and the journey usually takes about two hours. Despite this being a mission school, the headmaster at St Damians, Mr Gwejegweje, did not have a problem with unmarried staff bringing guests at night. In his opinion, it was better we did this sort of thing than begin to chase after the schoolgirls or the married women in the surrounding villages. Nevertheless, I respected Mr Gwejegweje, his wife and their two daughters, so I tried very hard to be discreet about what I was doing.

That night was fantastic! I have never encountered a woman that I was so compatible with, who took me to such heights, who showed me so many tricks and techniques, and who was also as responsive to mine the way it was with Aquilina that night. We eventually slept as the roosters began to crow. I woke up at around 10am, and Aquilina was gone. I searched for her throughout the house. As you know, out here in the rural areas, we do not lock our doors, even at night. I found it hard to accept that she had left the school premises. For one, the money I had paid her was still on top of the drawer where she had left it. I was struck by a startling thought: she had found something more valuable than the money. I searched thoroughly, but it looked like every moveable item in my house was still there. I checked the windows, and they were securely shut. Besides, there were flowers and vegetables planted under them outside so there would have been footprints and broken stalks. I asked my neighbours if they had seen a female stranger about, but no one could say they had seen her.

I realised that I had nothing to lose by giving her no further thought. She was gone. I did not know where she had come from. I had got what I had brought her to Tswakata for, so what more did I need, really? So, I spent the afternoon watching football at a local sports bar.

When I returned around sunset, I was astonished to find Aquilina waiting for me outside my house. I asked her where she had gone, and she said she had just popped out to see what the township was like and lost track of time. She had spent a lot of time at the bus station where, she said, she had bumped into a girl she had gone to school with, who was on her way to Marondera to take up a teaching post. After that, she had waded into a debate between a Rastafarian and some Jehovah's Witnesses. She had eaten, for she had money to buy both breakfast and lunch. I refrained from saying much. After all, we were not husband and wife that she had to give a detailed account of her movements. Even if she had been approached by other men, that had nothing to do with me. All the same, I was pleased that she had returned, and looked forward to another night of ecstasy.

We got into the house. Aquilina asked if she could stay a few days longer than what we had agreed on, until either I got tired of her or she figured out where she wanted to go next, whichever happened first. She was not expecting to get paid, but we could sleep together whenever I wanted, as she too had particularly enjoyed the previous night. And she could do the wifely chores around the house, the dishes, sweeping the house and cooking. But she fully understood that I was not her man and she was not my woman, and she had no expectation that she would eventually become my wife. How could I resist such an arrangement?

When I look back on this period, it seemed as if my heart was free of that hate I had harboured towards women. It was true that Aquilina had said that she was not expecting me to marry her, but what manner of compassion is it that moves a bachelor to wipe the snot off the nose of a single mother's child?[1] I thought the arrangement was good. Aquilina thought it was good. We had met along the way, but where

[1] Proverb, meaning people do not go out of their way to be nice without anticipating something in return.

she had come from and where she was going, she alone knew. That she was just a shameless prostitute, I was not so sure about. Even if she was, I was ready to believe that a person can reform. If I could eventually be cured of my mental problems, which made me hate all women, what could stop this young lady from deciding not to sell her body anymore? Even my own sister, Mati, after giving my manager all kinds of venereal diseases, was now a highly esteemed member of the women's group in her church. Were Mr Mavhura to publish that letter which moved me to attempt to commit suicide, no one would believe it had been written by her.

Sir, what people say, that a woman is medicine for the household, I got to witness it firsthand. My house transformed and became much more comfortable. My curtains had never been washed since I bought them when I moved to St Damian's. I thought they were light brown. When I saw them drying on the clothesline, I honestly thought Aquilina had gone out and bought new white ones!

What about her culinary skills? This lady performed wonders in the kitchen! We ate what I had always eaten in my house, but the way she made eggs, boerewors and kidneys was her unique method. Those days, I would be found licking my plate and the pots and other utensils. Aquilina found this uproariously funny, laughing like a girl. I went to work fed, my clothes clean and neatly ironed.

A week after we started living together thus, Aquilina said she needed to return to Harare to get the rest of her clothes at her paternal aunt's. Up until then, she had been making do with my T-shirts and jeans. I agreed to drive her there. We went to Harare in the evening, after I had finished work, and after we had eaten and made love. It was her idea that we travel in the evening. She said her aunt was a prostitute and lived alone, so Aquilina wanted to get there while the aunt was out and collect her things without getting into a conversation that could descend into a heated exchange. She had her own key to her aunt's place.

We returned to Chizhanje and parked near that same beerhall I had visited in search of hookers. When Aquilina stepped out of the vehicle, I was surprised to see her head off into the bushes behind the beerhall, where we had met, instead of towards the streets with houses on them. Perhaps there was a cluster of homes I did not know about. These days, there are so many housing projects springing up all over Harare. It was warm in the car, and I was a bit tired, so sleep soon seized me. Next thing I remember, Aquilina was back in the car beside me, shaking me on the shoulder. "I got my things, dear. Let's go!"

I turned and saw a large suitcase in the back seat. So, I started the car and we set off. When we got home, we got horizontal on the bed again, and I fell asleep. I woke up after midnight. It was only then I tried to process how Aquilina could have been back in the vehicle, for I was positive I had locked myself in when she had stepped out to go to her aunt's place. I have asked myself the question at least a hundred times since then! I never asked Aquilina herself. I just had this feeling that she would not appreciate the question at all.

Aquilina was still staying with me when the school term ended. Mr Gwejegweje, the headmaster, summoned me to his office. "See here, Maforimbo, I am afraid we won't be spending the holiday together. There is a situation in my family. A traditional situation. You being a youth, and a man of science, perhaps you might not understand such things.

41

The thing is that my daughters, Primrose and Precious have been having bad dreams and talking in their sleep. One thing they keep repeating is that they keep seeing a girl, a young woman. So, Mrs Gwejegweje and I have thought about taking the girls to the mountains. In Nyanga, there is to be found an expert traditional doctor who has helped us with such matters in the past. What this means for you, Maforimbo, is that you will hold the fort in my absence. I don't know when we will return, that doctor gets many patients from the four corners of the land. So, we might be away for the duration of the school holiday.

The headmaster often requested some of the teachers to stay on over the school holiday to help with administrative stuff, attend meetings with officials from the Ministry of Education and other organisations. There was extra pay from the ministry, and even more out of the school, or, rather, the church which ran it. I had already agreed to remain over the holiday but was surprised to be left in charge of the school. This was indeed a great honour, to be chosen above other teachers, all of whom had been at the school for longer than me. I thanked Mr Gwejegweje profusely.

Talk eventually turned to other matters. He asked me about the girl I had mentioned to him. Mr Gwejegweje looked surprised to learn that Aquilina had been staying with me for about three months now. He laughed and said, "Well, it looks to me like it's going to happen at last. I shall send my suit to the dry cleaners!"

"You really think so, Mr Gwejegweje?" I was sceptical, but I was filled with happiness.

"Can't you see that you've already started a household, eh, Maforimbo? You should come round to the house and introduce her to Mrs Gwejegweje. You see, Maforimbo, these families start in different ways. What makes them endure is the couple showing each other commitment. All that remains now is for you to take that initiative as a man and begin the due process to let her people know that this is what you, as a couple, have decided to become."

The fact of the matter was that our relationship, Aquilina and I, worked perfectly for me! We found each other compatible in so many ways, we liked the same music and singers, movies and actors, and even the same books. Of things to talk about, was there any end? Aquilina said she had done her 'A' Levels, but she had not garnered enough points to be admitted into university. But she was very intellectual. She was not very strong in the sciences, but it was through her knowledge of world history and literature that I began to appreciate their value in everyday life. We were fortunate that our school had loads of books, donated by well-wishers abroad. Aquilina introduced me to Shakespeare, the sisters Brontë, and other English writers whose works are loved the world over. She exposed me to Zimbabwean and other African writers of fiction, such as Dambudzo Marechera, Yvonne Vera, Bessie Head, and others. We ate from the same plate and drank from the same glass. It was as if we had been together for years. When it came to physical intimacy, we did not wait for night time or need to be in the bedroom. The bathroom, the kitchen, all rooms were suitable. Most of the time, Aquilina wore nothing but a pair of panties.

The day schools closed for the holiday, I took Aquilina to Harare, to introduce her to Mati. She advised me to inform our maternal uncles about her. They would know the next steps to take in observing tradition. I am telling you all this, sir, because I want you to see my state of mind and my plans before I killed Aquilina. I loved her enough to want to marry her.

The day before yesterday, I left Aquilina in bed, sleeping, and set off for Tswakata. I needed to see this guy who I thought could hire out his truck at a knock-down rate. There is a mine that has gone bankrupt recently and was desperate to liquidate its assets quickly rather than continue to pay for their storage. I was thinking of launching a transport business. There were many former civil servants in the area who had recently been made redundant under the Economic Structural Adjustment Programme, who were now engaged in horticulture, selling their produce to Harare and Marondera. Their biggest challenge was transporting their produce, so I thought I had a regular and lucrative market there.

When I got to this guy, Stanford's garage, there were some other guys just lazing about under the trees behind the garage. We pooled our money and bought a couple of scuds,[1] and just hung out, drinking and chatting. It was towards sunset that we finally discussed the truck I had come to see him about. Indeed, he had a truck available and at a rate agreeable to me. I promised to return with a cheque for the deposit.

As I approached the cluster of teacher's houses at St Damian's, I saw Mr Gwejegweje leave mine. It was dark, but I recognised his distinct frame and gait. He looked this way and that, as if to ensure that there was no one watching him, before he headed towards his house. I had the impression that he had paused to hitch up his trousers.

---

[1] A commercialised version of the traditional opaque beer, so named because it came out during the Gulf war.

When I got into the house, Aquilina greeted me with a kiss, as always. She said nothing about Mr Gwejegweje. I did not say anything either. But conflicting thoughts swirled in my head.

The next day, meaning yesterday, Mr Gwejegweje came to the house to hand over the keys before embarking on his trip to Nyanga. Aquilina was in the backyard, putting clothes on the line to dry. I called her, hoping to get her to bring us some drinks, but she never came. But I could hear her singing to herself in the backyard.

"Never mind the young lady, Maforimbo," said Mr Gwejegweje. "You know what they say; a woman's work is never done, especially around the house. Besides, you and I both have hands, I don't think you are incapable of going to the fridge and getting us drinks, man! I will come back another day, and then I will look forward to a full meal. But I will send word in advance, so that I don't find her too busy with household duties."

After I returned from the kitchen with a couple of bottles of ice-cold lager, Mr Gwejegweje told me why he had come. "See here, Maforimbo. The reason I came here with the keys myself, instead of sending Pri or Pre, is that Gwisai rang me this morning. He says he landed himself a job in Botswana as a research assistant at a mining company. This means he will not be returning next term. So, I was thinking that you should take his place for now as the Head of the Science Department, at least until my superiors find someone substantive or they decide whether you should remain in the position. But I don't think it will prove too hard to persuade the board to give you the position permanently. With your track record so far, it was always going to be yours at some point. Even Gwisai himself, when you first came here, said that you were his heir apparent."

I did not know what to say. I did not know whether to show surprise or delight at the news. I burst into laughter, then clamped a palm across my mouth. Then, I tried to grab Mr Gwejegweje's hand so that I could shake it. All this time, I was yelling for Aquilina to come in and hear the good news. She never came. She was still singing her song, outside. Mr Gwejegweje finally downed his beer and rose. "I have to get going, Maforimbo. We have to reach Harare before the stores close. We shall go to Mutare by the evening train from there, and proceed by bus to Nyanga."

By the time Mr Gwejegweje left, I could no longer contain myself. I was jumping up and down and clapping my hands. I went to the kitchen to see what it was exactly that Aquilina had not been able to tear herself from. The door from the kitchen to the backyard was wide open, but I did not see her. Even the clothes she had been hanging on the line were no longer there. I stepped out into the backyard and walked towards the front of the house.

Aquilina was standing at the gate, talking to Mr Gwejegweje. I thought she had seen him leave the house and had walked him to the gate. As she spoke, Mr Gwejegweje grinned lasciviously at her. Then his hand fell on her shoulder, and slid down slowly, caressingly, until he reached her waist and circled to her back, while still sliding down. I felt a flaming rage rise from my heart until it burned all over my entire being. I found myself staggering as I stomped back into the house and slumped into a sofa. One thought held my consciousness: *Aquilina, really?* The room seemed to spin.

The spinning stopped abruptly. Aquilina had entered the lounge, her hands wet from handling the clothes she had been hanging outside. She wore a T-shirt that clung wetly to her breasts, and a wrapper that hugged her hips, held together by a knot just under her navel. Seeing my face, her smile faded. "What's the matter, darling?" she asked. "Why were you yelling my name like that?"

I did not reply right away. I opened my mouth, but the seething rage had got my voice. Aquilina moved closer and planted herself on the arm of the sofa I sat on. How was she to know she was now signing her death warrant?

"Hati, what is the matter, darling?" she asked again, and tried to touch me. I moved away. She looked surprised by this.

"I see you get along very well with Mr Gwejegweje," I seethed.

Nothing more needed to be said. Her eyes told me everything. Everything I suspected, she confirmed it all with the way she looked at me. I knew that look all too well. I had seen it in the eyes of so many women I had come across in my life.

I rose. "So, you think it's stupidity on my part? You are sleeping with Mr Gwejegweje, aren't you? You are a little whore, you hear me? Little whore! Women, all of you are whores!"

It was then she realised the danger she was in. She tried to back away, but she was on the sofa, and I stood over her. Looking down on her, seeing her terror, I suddenly realised what had been happening in my life ever since she came in it. She was behind my being made Acting Headmaster at St Damian's. It was her who had seen to my promotion as Acting Head of the Science Department. Aquilina was the payment I had not given you, Mr Gwejegweje! As had my sister, Aquilina had played the harlot to enhance my position on the job!

With both hands, I clenched her extensions and wound them around her neck. I saw the panic in her eyes as she raised her arms to fight me, but it was too late. The colour drained from her face, her eyes bulged and her mouth gaped, a gurgling noise issuing from it, but I tightened my stranglehold. Her face transformed into that of Mother, of Mati, of Grandmother, of Emilia and Aunty Mai Berita, of every woman I had ever met in my life, every woman I hated for being disloyal, every woman I did not get the chance to punish with my own hand.

I pulled her close and kissed her. With my mouth, I felt her soul leave her body and the cold creep in. I pushed her back onto the sofa, her head lolling like that of a drunk. I stared at her for a long time afterwards.

I regret that I do not clearly remember much of what happened after that up to the moment I came here and surrendered myself to you. But I do remember digging a grave in the bushes behind the teachers' houses. I remember too casting Aquilina's body in that pit and covering it with soil. I wrote her name on top with pebbles. I think I worked all night. It being a holiday, I don't think anyone saw me. At sunrise, I came here and told the police of my crime, of murdering Aquilina.

I, Hatifari Maforimbo, swear that this statement I have given is, to the best of my knowledge, true. Furthermore, I swear that I understood what has been explained to me, that if I am found to have written falsehoods, I am liable to punishment by law.

Signed: *Hmaforimbo*
Date:19/08/97

CHAPTER 2
Interlude

Being a collection of documents related to the signed confession of Hatifari Maforimbo.

8956 Kuwadzana Extension
Harare

13 May 1996

Dear Hati

My dear brother, I am so full of praise to the Lord right now! Uncle Tau was here, and he told me that you are getting better and will soon be leaving that ward! Bless and Justin have kept me up to date with things, maybe you will see them later this week!

It has been two whole years since I last saw you, my only real brother! Dr Zwelani said it was for the best. I was really hurt, but I can see now that it had to be this way! She phoned me today and told me that you had made a full recovery. I am so happy, I cried and praised Jesus for His intervention. Yes, you may say it was the psychiatrist, but who gives the psychiatrist the knowledge and skill to discover how unclean spirits torment an innocent soul, who gives them the power to drive them away? When we meet, we shall argue about this, me with my Jesus and you and your science!

So much has happened in the last two years. I was delivered from my life of sin, and today I stand as a woman of God! After you fell ill, I had to sit down and really think about my life, and I knew that I had to find God. I first went to Uncle Amos' church, but I was not welcome there, because one of the elders used to be a friend of mine. I do not deny my past sins, but they judged me for them. And to think they were actually led by this very same elder that I committed those sins with! Never mind.

But Jesus was still looking for His lost sheep, and he found me at the Royal Tent Ministries. I cannot describe that moment when I repented and a new, clean spirit came over me, Hati! I am a different person now. That woman who brought you shame is gone. Since then, it has been blessing upon blessing!

At Royal Tent Ministries, I found my God-fearing man, your brother-in-law, Herenimo Ncube. But you have been told all this already, so let me not go into it. Here is a picture of the three of us, with your lovely niece, Busiso. Heri thinks she will be a great scientist one day, like her uncle.

Please write back soon, my dear brother, and let me know when you can come to stay with us. Our home is humble, but it has the unseen riches of the Son of King Solomon!

Your loving sister
Mati

PS: I had to check with Dr Zwelani before adding this bit, but she says you are fine and can be told these things.

There is one thing Uncle Tau and the boys will not have told you, because only I have that information. I found out last year that our father died in 1992, not long after I tried to contact him and he chased me out of his workplace like a dog. He was one of the first people to be diagnosed with HIV in this country. In fact, all of his siblings and most of his extended family succumbed to the disease, and this is why I was unable to track him down all this time. You may be the last of the Maforimbos, Hati.

Ward 14, Psychiatry Unit
Harare Central Hospital
PO Box CY37698
Causeway
Harare

14 May 1996

My dear sister

Thanks for your letter, it really made me happy! I know and understand why you did not come to see me. That I am able to say this now shows how much I have got a grip on reality. What happened in the past is in the past, and I do not want you to keep thinking that it is your fault that I lost my mind. Dr Zwelani has shown me that what happened can happen to anyone, what is important is to be able to move on from such things.

I will be leaving this place next week. I would really love to come straight to yours and meet my brother-in-law and my niece, but that will have to wait. Perhaps Justin did not tell you because he wanted it to be my news, but Uncle Tau got me a job at a school in Arcturus or Goromonzi, somewhere just outside Harare, off Mutare Road. I think Uncle Tau went to school with one of the senior teachers there and got him to put in a good word for me. Since it's already term-time, I should get started right away.

I will come and see you over the school holiday in August. Please let me know when you will be in the country. With Justin and Blessing also out of Harare, you are the only reason I have for returning to the city that has so many painful memories for me. But don't worry, the pain is now safely buried deep down by the new sense of purpose that Dr Zwelani (and your prayers!!!) worked so hard to guide me towards.

I will let you know about this school in my next letter. Greetings to everyone

Your loving brother
Hati

The Mabuu

Monday, May 15, 1997

The Ripper of Chizhanje?

Fear stalks the ladies of the night in the Chizhanje area after the body of a prostitute was found last week, the victim of a gruesome murder. Police are still investigating.

"The police are saying that it was an isolated case," said one self-confessed sex worker, who declined to give her name, "but most of us girls believe we have a Jack The Ripper in our midst!" She was referring to the notorious serial killer who targeted prostitutes in Victorian London. It is not an unreasonable comparison, as there have been many such cases around the world of a serial killer targeting the ladies of the night.

"We will die like animals, and the police will do nothing, because we do not matter," said another sex worker, who only gave her name as Mavis.

However, both the police and bar owners in the area have emphatically denied that sex workers are not valued as human beings. "Those girls bring in the customers," said Mrs Makona, proprietor of Makona's

Rer
foll
imp

The
that
rela
the
beh
of a
exp
in li
its
beh
con
or v

It m
tota
thin
dec
mos

53

St Damian's Secondary School
PO Box 17
Tswakata Township
Goromonzi

30 May 1997

My dear Taurai

First, let me say thank you very much for the books! Please thank your American friends for me. Let me know in advance when they are coming over, we would love to host them as a school so they can see the impact of their generosity. And you must come over soon, it has been a while since Mai Prim and I have seen you. Besides, you have another reason to come over – the young man you sent me.

Mr Maforimbo is a pedagogue par excellent! He not only knows his physics, chemistry and biology, but also how to teach it. There are kids here who were just muddling through, coming as they do from a culture where the only things worth learning in school are those that can lead to a job in the city. Thanks to Maforimbo, these children can now see how learning about polymers and magnetic fields can be applied to their peasant farm life. One girl has started to make soap at home and plans to set up a soap-making business with some of the women in the community. Another girl has made something that explodes, not sure what future there is in that. Perhaps she dreams of Zimbabwe becoming a military power!

I could go on and on, but I have already praised your nephew every time we meet. And I will say it again, he deserves to progress beyond teaching at a school in the rural area. He should be at one of those big pharmaceuticals, leading the quest to find a cure for AIDS.

Anyways, a few days ago, Maforimbo came to see me. He told me he has a girl who appears to have moved in with him. He thought it proper and respectful to let me know, but I told him what my teachers do in their homes and outside of school hours is their business. I'd prefer the unmarried ones have live-in girlfriends than to start messing about with the students.

If the relationship is going anywhere, you, being the uncle, will be told in due course. I am only giving you a heads-up because you asked me to keep an eye on Maforimbo, in light of his recent mental illness. I am no expert, Tau, old buddy, but I think having a steady girlfriend is a good sign of his recovery. There was even a rumour that he frequents the beerhalls to pick up prostitutes, but I have never seen evidence of this. This live-in should quash such rumours.

I haven't seen her yet, but Maforimbo says she is very beautiful, and cooks and cleans. You can see it on his face that she has stolen his heart! However, I have to say that at this stage, only he knows of her beauty and her cooking and cleaning skills. When you walk past his house, the curtains still look dirty!

Anyways, I have got to rush now. I need to see Mrs Magura, our main History teacher. She is worried about her dog, which disappeared a few days ago. It's possible it was stolen. Very peculiar business, if you ask me. I have never heard of a pet dog that would be useless for hunting, being stolen.

My regards to Mai Berita.

Your loving friend
Stannie

CHAPTER 3
The Testimonies

ZIMBABWE REPUBLIC POLICE - MASHONALAND EAST COMMAND

STATEMENT FORM

GIVEN NAME: Oliver Stanislaus

FAMILY NAME: Gwejegweje

NAME PREVIOUSLY HELD (IF DIFFERENT FROM ABOVE): N/A

DATE OF BIRTH: 11/04/53

NATIONAL IDENTITY NUMBER: 63-86602933-T-58

ADDRESS: St Damian's Secondary School, PO Box 17, Tswakata Township

DISTRICT: Goromonzi

TELEPHONE NUMBER: (730) 5441

ABOUT THE STATEMENT:

Place where written: TSAKWATA POLICE STATION
Date: 19 August 1997
Time: 16:45

STATEMENT

I, Oliver Stanislaus Gwejegweje, being the Headmaster at Damian's Secondary School here in Tswakata, wish to make the following known in relation to Hatifari Maforimbo and the events leading to his arrest.

1. On the 26th of May this year, Hatifari Maforimbo, one of the teachers under me, came to me and asked if his new female companion could stay with him in the accommodation provided to him at St Damian's. He said this young lady was called Aquilina, and she came from Harare. I told him that I had no problem with the arrangement. However, I want to state categorically that not once did I actually see this young lady in person.

2. When I asked him further about this Aquilina, the first time I was told she had gone to Mutoko to see her aunt. On another occasion, I was told she had gone to Hwedza, where a friend of hers lived.

3. Whenever I went to Maforimbo's house, I was told that Aquilina was in another room and was too busy to even take a break, greet visitors or prepare refreshments for them, or I would be told that she had just gone out to the shops, and I had just missed her. This is what happened on the 16th of this month, when I went over to Maforimbo's house to tell him of my decision to promote him to Acting Head of the Department of Science. I did not see this Aquilina, but Maforimbo told me that she was outside, hanging laundry.

4. I want to state that, as someone who took Mr Maforimbo as if he were my own younger brother, I am deeply concerned about his arrest and murder charge I am most upset that he would say that I was having an affair with his girlfriend! I am anxious that such words will tarnish my name in society, as I am held in high esteem here in Tswakata as a headmaster, as a father of two daughters and as a

Christian, who has preached occasionally at St
Damian's.

I, Oliver Stanislaus Gwejegweje, swear that this statement
that I have written down is, to the best of my knowledge,
true. Furthermore, I swear that I understood what has been
explained to me, that if I am found to have written
falsehoods, I am liable to punishment by law.

Signed: *OSGwejegweje*
Date: 21/08/97

ZIMBABWE REPUBLIC POLICE -
MASHONALAND EAST COMMAND

STATEMENT FORM

GIVEN NAME: Matilda Zvamaida

FAMILY NAME: Ncube

NAME PREVIOUSLY HELD (IF DIFFERENT FROM ABOVE): Maforimbo

DATE OF BIRTH: 23/06/71

NATIONAL IDENTITY NUMBER: 63-27775971-K-34

ADDRESS: 15 Muskgrove Avenue, Malbereign West, Harare

DISTRICT: Harare

TELEPHONE NUMBER: (04) 309222

ABOUT THE STATEMENT:

Place where written: TSAKWATA POLICE STATION

Date: 19 August 1997

Time: 21:40

STATEMENT

1. I am the older sister of Hatifari Maforimbo, who is currently helping police with their enquiries into the murder of Aquilina.

On the 6th of August, Hatifari came to my house to introduce his new girlfriend. Prior to this, he had telephoned to say he wanted to introduce me to the lady he wished to marry. We had not had the opportunity to meet before because my husband and I are often out of the country on trips to sell various items and to purchase things to sell here in Zimbabwe. We are also very busy with church.

However, when he came to my home, I did not see any girl in his car. I told him that I could not see anyone, after which he became angry. Fearing what might have happened next, I began to pretend as if I could see her, this Aquilina, and invited her into the house.

It was almost like playing house. I pretended to see and talk to Aquilina, and we had tea with her. But I testify that during the entire visit, we were alone, my brother and I.

Hatifari once had a mental breakdown and spent two years in an institution. It is my view that this Aquilina only exists in Hatifari's imagination, and that he is having a relapse of his mental illness. After he left, I prayed fervently. I told our maternal uncles, and they said we had to wait and see if his illness would adversely impact his work, and if it did, then they would see the need to intervene as a family. However, I wish to reiterate that in all my life, I have never laid eyes on anyone called Aquilina, and I do not believe that such a person exists.

I, Matilda Zvamaida Maforimbo-Ncube, swear that this statement that I have written down is, to the best of my knowledge, true. Furthermore, I swear that I understood what has been explained to me, that if I am found to have written falsehoods, I am liable to punishment by law.

Signed: MZN~cube~
Date: 19/08/97

ZIMBABWE REPUBLIC POLICE - MASHONALAND EAST COMMAND

STATEMENT FORM

GIVEN NAME: Taurayi

FAMILY NAME: Kaumbe

NAMES PREVIOUSLY HELD (IF DIFFERENT FROM ABOVE): N/A

DATE OF BIRTH: 11/*03*/*52*

NATIONAL IDENTITY NUMBER: *63-64775971-K-34*

ADDRESS: 119 St Patricks Drive, Gallant Park, Harare

DISTRICT: Harare

TELEPHONE NUMBER: (04) 3046512

ABOUT THE STATEMENT:

Place where written: TSAKWATA POLICE STATION

Date: 19 August 1997

Time: 23:30

STATEMENT

I am the elder maternal uncle of Hatifari Maforimbo and his siblings. His mother and maternal grandparents are deceased, and he has no contact with his father or his father's side of the family, which leaves me in loco parentis.

In response to the questions posed to me by the police officers at this station, I state that what I know of the lady called Aquilina, who is the subject of this enquiry, is what has been told to me by my nephew, his sister, Mrs

Ncube, and the Headmaster of St Damians, Mr Gwejegweje, who is an old friend of mine.

I first heard of Aquilina at the end of May this year, when Mr Gwejegweje reported in a letter that my nephew had informed him he had a girl who had just moved in with him and sought his approval as the headmaster for such an arrangement. Mr Gwejegweje saw it fit to tell me right away because he is aware of my nephew's history of mental illness. It was because of our friendship that he gave Hati a post at the school so soon after leaving the psychiatric unit at Harare Central Hospital. Given the attitudes towards former mental patients, it is unlikely Hati would have got a job anywhere else. In fact, in reporting this development, Mr Gwejegweje hoped I would see what he saw; a sign that Hati had recovered enough to enter a relationship. This is how I interpreted the news. My friend, Gwejegweje, mentioned in passing that he had not actually seen Aquilina yet, but he hoped he would soon. At any rate, if there was to be a future in the relationship, it was to be expected that Hati would contact me as I would have a role to play in the customary procedures.

In July this year, Hati telephoned me from a callbox and told me about Aquilina. He asked me if I could speak to her. To my bewilderment, when he said he put her on the phone, I could not hear anyone. At first, I thought she was being shy, or there was a technical fault with the phone. But I could hear my nephew laughing in the background and talking to someone. He even told her to ask me about my work with the Ministry of Mines. I was very confused. I was shouting, "Hullo?!" into the phone, and my colleagues in the office were starting to look at me as if I was mad. Then Hatifari came on and asked me what I thought of Aquilina.

Before I could answer, he said they were coming to see me soon, and that was that.

I forgot about this incident until early this month, when I got a call from my niece, Mrs Matilda Ncube, Hatifari's older sister. She told me that he had just been to her house to introduce Aquilina. To her surprise, Hatifari had come alone but acted as if Aquilina was present! He talked to Aquilina, laughed at her jokes etc, but Matilda could only see him. She told me she was only relieved her husband was out, as she would not have wanted him to see her brother in such a state. We are both convinced that Hatifari was having another episode of his mental illness, although I do not remember if he ever experienced hallucinations before.

Based on the above, I am convinced that Aquilina is a product of my nephew's mental illness. The police have found no body in the alleged grave, and none of the people Hatifari has told about her have actually seen this Aquilina.

I, Taurayi Kaumbe, swear that this statement that I have written down is, to the best of my knowledge, true. Furthermore, I swear that I understood what has been explained to me, that if I am found to have written falsehoods, I am liable to punishment by law.

Witness' Signature: *TKaumbe*
Date: 19/08/97

ZIMBABWE REPUBLIC POLICE - MASHONALAND EAST PROVINCIAL

COMMAND CASE REPORTS

TSWAKATA DISTRICT
NUMBER: VT 19/08/97/1012
INCIDENT: Murder
OFFICER REPORTING: Detective Lawrence Kweche
Date: 19 August 1997

1. At 11:23 this morning, a man called Hatifari Maforimbo came to Tswakata Police Station. He showed me his ID, which confirms this is indeed his name and that he was born in Harare in 1973. He gave me his address as St Damian's Secondary School, PO Box 17, Tswakata Township.

2. Maforimbo states that in July of this year, he met a young lady by the name of Aquilina near the council beerhall in the neighbourhood of Chizhanje, Mabvuku, in the city of Harare, and brought her to Tswakata with the intention of engaging in prostitution, following which, they would go their separate ways the next day. He states that he does not know Aquilina's full name.

3. Maforimbo states that his encounter with Aquilina did not end that evening. They agreed that she would stay at his given address, which was the case until yesterday, 18 August, when, according to

66

Maforimbo, he murdered Aquilina and buried her behind his house at the address he has given.

4. I went to the address in question in the company of two constables, Gavanga and Nduna. Behind the house, outside the yard, on a clearing leading to the open savannah, we found a mound of earth adorned with pebbles arranged to form the name AQUILINA. We scooped up the earth, and dug into the ground until we reached bedrock, but we did not find a body. Indeed, there is no evidence at all that anything had been placed under that mound of earth.

5. With my fellow policemen, we searched the entire house, but we did not find any physical evidence to substantiate Maforimbo's statement of the events he alleged had transpired there. Indeed, we spoke to several persons who reside at the mission school, but none of them could say they had ever seen Aquilina, or any female at the house that we could reasonably assume to be Aqulina. To all appearances, Mr Maforimbo has been alone at the house.

6. The Headmaster of St Damian's Secondary School, a Mr Gwejegweje, has also written a statement. Mr Gwejegweje stated that he did not see anyone else apart from Maforimbo when he went to the house to inform him about a Mr Gwisai, who had ceased to be a teacher at St Damian's Secondary School. He is particularly upset that Maforimbo would claim

that he was sexually involved with Aquilina.

7. Mr and Mrs Kapito, who live in the house across from Maforimbo's, have stated that they have never seen Aquilina. However, Mrs Kapito says that she has heard gossip at the local shops that a young lady has been occasionally seen leaning against the wall of the bar. This girl was said to be scary because she did not speak to anyone. Mrs Kapito added that her neighbour's dog had run away in May, and that the children at that house had begun to have nightmares.

8. I have discussed this case with Mr Simbisai Mugodhi, the District Prosecutor. He is of the view that as police have not recovered a body, and there appears to be no evidence that there ever existed this person called Aquilina, his office did not see the usefulness of proceeding with this case to a trial. For these reasons, he has advised us to refer Maforimbo to a psychiatrist.

EXCERPTS FROM HATIFARI MAFORIMBO'S FORENSIC PSYCHIATRIC EVALUATION

HARARE EAST PSYCHIATRIC CENTRE

41 Mupangara Drive
Old Mabvuku
Harare
Phone: (04) 49684041-7
Fax: (04) 496840414

23rd August 1997

ATT: Detective Lawrence Kweche

Z.R.P. - Tswakata
PO Box 73
Tswakata

Re: <u>Mr Hatifari Maforimbo, DOB: 11 February 1973</u>

I, <u>Dr Nobuhle Zwelani</u>, ZPS # 43/94, of <u>Harare East Psychiatric Centre,</u> testify as follows:
- I am a psychiatrist authorised to practise in the Republic of Zimbabwe by law, and by the regulations of the Zimbabwe Psychiatric Council.
- I hold the following academic qualifications: Master of Community Psychology (University of Chitungwiza, 1995), Bachelor of Psychiatry (University of Chitungwiza, 1991), Bachelor of

Medicine (University of Zimbabwe, 1987).
- I started practice here at Harare East Psychiatric Centre in 1992.

Detective Kweche of Tswakata Police Station requested for me to provide a psychiatric evaluation of one Hatifari Maforimbo [M;24], who is a former patient of mine at Harare Central Hospital. Following my evaluation, Hatifari is now receiving treatment at this clinic.

As I have had the opportunity to interview Mr Maforimbo, and being satisfied from said interview that Mr Maforimbo has no Capacity (Mental Health Act, 2000) at this stage, I have foregone seeking Mr Maforimbo's consent before presenting this report to the police.

This Report is compiled from:
> 1. Notes made during my examination of Hatifari from when he was first admitted to the Psychiatric Unit at Harare Central in 1994, following his attempt to commit suicide, which form part of his permanent medical record.
> 2. Notes made during my examination when he was brought to this clinic this morning.

PATIENT DESCRIPTION:
This is a young man of twenty-four years.

DIAGNOSIS:
Axis I: Post-traumatic stress disorder, chronic.
Axis II: Antisocial personality disorder, borderline personality disorder.

Axis V: Brief Psychiatric Rating Scale is at 75.

The patient has stated that he has experienced several traumatic incidents throughout his childhood. He exhibits a pathological hatred of women.

HISTORY OF PATIENT:

Hatifari Maforimbo has a history of mental health problems since his teenage years, which remained undiagnosed but saw him exhibit violent behaviour that saw him excluded from both secondary school and university. He has not informed me of any other serious health conditions or injuries. I have seen documentation that confirms that he has undergone all mandatory immunisation procedures.

The patient has stated that he had an unhappy childhood. His parents divorced when he was seven years old, after his mother was found in a compromising position with another man. He was raised by his mother, who had been sent away from the matrimonial home with her children, Hatifari and his sister Matilda, and went to live with her parents in another part of Harare. Over the years, there were many incidents which exposed his mother's sexual promiscuity, which filled Hatifari with a strong sense of shame and prevented him from forming healthy relationships with his peers at a time when such interaction was crucial to forming a healthy mental outlook. He was bullied and teased by his peers because of his mother's scandalous reputation. Attending a boarding secondary school in another part of the country only made him realise how widespread his mother's infamy was. He seriously injured a peer at boarding school, who had provoked him by singing a lewd song about his mother, and was promptly expelled. Hatifari had to continue his education at a local school, something considered a "step down" socially, further entrenching his sense of humiliation. He was later expelled from university after seriously injuring a female peer. He found out that his sister had been having an affair with the father of one of her peers.

These incidents prompted him to contemplate suicide.

MENTAL HEALTH HISTORY

- In 1988, while at secondary school, Hatifari stabbed a fellow student in the eye with a spoon, resulting in a life-changing injury.
- In 1993, while at university, Hatifari assaulted a fellow student and fractured her left eye-socket. She was part of a group of activists advocating for the right of female students to wear what they wanted without fear of verbal or physical attacks by those who disapprove of such clothing.
- In 1994, Hatifari attempted to commit suicide by leaping in front of an oncoming train. This was after learning he only got his job at a chemicals factory in Chitungwiza because his sister had agreed to have sex with the manager in exchange. It was following this incident that he was first admitted to this hospital. He was treated here for two years.

FAMILY HISTORY OF MENTAL ILLNESS

There is no known history of mental illness among all of Hatifari's known close relatives.

OTHER HEALTH PROBLEMS/DISABILITIES

No physical medical ailments have been observed on Hatifari, nor has he reported any.

Hatifari has no known disability which prevents him from or restricts his performance of the same daily tasks as most people.

PERSONAL LIFE & RELATIONSHIPS

Hatifari does not have a partner or child. He has two sisters and three younger brothers. His mother is deceased, and he last saw his father as an infant. He does not know where his father is, but states he believes his sister, Mrs Ncube, has had contact with him. He has stated that he has not had a "proper" girlfriend. His first relationship as a teenager ended when he found out the girl was sleeping with a local businessman after she had been assaulted by the businessman's wife. He regards "Aquilina" as his first serious girlfriend.

FORENSIC HISTORY

Hatifari has confessed to murdering his live-in girlfriend, who is known only as "Aquilina," having gone of his own will to the police. However, the police state they have not recovered any substantial evidence to show a crime has been committed, or that the alleged victim ever existed or still exists as a real person, or that anything else is known about this matter beyond Hatifari's given testimony. Accordingly, the Prosecutor has decided not to proceed to a trial for the alleged murder and has asked that Hatifari be examined by a psychiatrist.

HISTORY OF SUBSTANCE MISUSE

Hatifari admitted to smoking marijuana from time to time since his teenage years but feels he has reduced his consumption. He drinks moderately on weekends. He is also in the habit of visiting different bars, seeking the company of prostitutes.

HEALTH RISKS

I have not identified anything that I could consider as a physical health risk to Hatifari, apart from the likelihood of contracting an STD. However, this risk becomes unlikely if he is detained for treatment for his mental condition.

It is my assessment that there is little risk of attempted suicide. Although he is distressed, the patient does not regret the crime he believes he has committed.

Nevertheless, there is a risk of relapsing to his previous pathological misogyny and acting this out through violence towards women, which may include murder.

He has not reported seeing any hallucinations since coming here. In his mind, he accepts that "Aquilina" is gone because he believes that he killed her.

The patient understands that he is to be treated for a mental health condition. However, he believes he is being treated only for his misogyny, and not for the memories he holds of "Aquilina." Hatifari is persistent in his belief that "Aquilina" was a real person and that he killed her.

ASSESSMENT

Hatifari witnessed his mother engage in licentious behaviour, which led to the break-up of his family, and he grew up without contact with his father. His sister was expelled from school after it came to light that she was having an affair with a peer's father. Following this, his sister had a reputation in the community for sexual promiscuity. His first girlfriend was caught having sexual relations with a well-known businessman. This girlfriend was viciously attacked by the wife of that businessman and her friends, who pushed a Coke bottle into her vagina. Given the patient's history, it is reasonable to believe this is what led to his perception of women as "evil" and thereafter, the justification of the use of violence as a form of punishment. Prior to that, his anger and violence were directed at people who mocked him about his mother, but he might have come around to blaming her as the cause of the humiliation he felt.

7 Maruva Crescent
Zengeza 3
Chitungwiza

15 September 1997

My friend, Kweche

Do you suppose I slept? I could not stop thinking about this case you sent me! Truly, the dead never saw anything!

Really, that statement of his is most fascinating!

Well, if there is no corpse, and if the doctor is convinced this fellow is not well, there is not much you can do except let him go. You can't charge him with the murder of someone you cannot even show existed, can you?

By the way, my friend, does your sister-in-law still travel frequently to Mozambique? The missus has developed a craving for prawns these days. God knows which of those women get-togethers she sampled them at, now she basically lives off them! I tried to explain to her that like the catfish she loathes, prawns are among the aquatic creatures listed in the Bible as unclean, but she says if that is the case, she will gladly go to hell, then!!! So please, if you can, organise some for me. I strongly suspect that prawns are "the thing" your missus referred to.

Have you heard the latest from Chimbetu? Musoni said he heard it played at Ziko, he was there with that school teacher he has been seeing a lot of lately! If he hasn't told you about her himself, then I shall say no more, except to advise you to buy a nice suit, my friend! Get a nice outfit for Mai Cindy, complete with a hat, because later this year, it is going to be eventful. That teacher has stolen Musoni's heart!

I will try to catch you on the phone, perhaps when the network has been fixed. They are crazy, these mobile phone company boys. You should lock them up every weekend, that will teach them! (just joking)

Your friend,

O. Sambiri

PS: About the new W.P.C at your station, I would rather you forgot about the matter! Are you not aware of this disease which has finished nearly everyone off? Where is your brother today? Are you not the one looking after the four children he left behind? Now if you go looking for it, who is going to look after both your kids? Let it shake and quiver in those tight pants, while you remain in good health, and you get to see your children finish school!!

EPILOGUE

From: "Larry Kweche" <zvesekweche@barnford.gov.uk>
To: "Onesimus Sambiri" <sambirio@zimmail.co.zw>
Date: 24 October 2011, 2:43 p.m

Subject: FW: AQUILINA

Hezvo[1]*!* Have a read of this shocker coming out of
Harare! The plot thickens. I don't know, you're the one who
is still a detective in Zimbabwe. I had actually forgotten
about the case of Hatifari Maforimbo, just as I have
forgotten so many of the cases that I investigated during my
time in the force.

I think this is a case for those Rasta private detectives you
always talk about. Or, should we refer it to ZINATHA[2] first?

---------- FORWARDED MESSAGE ----------

From: Nyasha Zulu <Niashazoulou@gmail.com>
To: Larry Kweche" <zvesekweche@barnford.gov.uk>
Date: Tuesday, October 24, 2011 2:16 PM
Subject: AQUILINA
📎 **Aquilina.jpeg**
Father of Cindy, we have here a situation that could have
come out of that old TV series, *The Twilight Zone!*

Do you remember that case you told me about, when we
were still at Tswakata, of that young man who came in on his
own and confessed to having killed his live-in girlfriend. I
was still stationed in Lupane when it happened, but the story

[1] In interjection of amazement, literal
translation unavailable.
[2] Zimbabwe National Traditional Healers
Association, the professional regulatory body
for practitioners of traditional medicine and
non-Christian faith healers.

79

was still topical when I was transferred to Tswakata. The chap, the "murderer", was called Maforimbo, Hatifari Maforimbo, and the girl – if there ever was a girl – was called Aqulina?

It turns out Maforimbo left us just last year. He never got better, unfortunately. He was discharged from the mental hospital and went to live with his sister, here in Harare. His brother-in-law is into the church thing, so he tried to dispel what he believed to be evil spirits haunting Maforimbo. In fact, Hatifari's picture is still on the church website, with a caption saying he was cured of his mental health problems through prayer. However, the truth is he actually got worse, and began to use hard drugs. They say it never rains but pours! It is reported that his sister became ill – AIDS – and died, leaving him with no one to provide him with the proper care he needed. I believe he has other siblings, some now in South Africa while one is in Botswana, but it seems they were not close.

One day, he just left the house and went to the railway line, where he threw himself into an approaching train. Perhaps this sad incident was featured in the papers, and you might have seen it online, but I don't recall seeing anything myself. I have asked someone to look it up.

Boss, I don't know if you saw on one of the online newspapers a few months ago, a story about a body which was found in the Chizhanje area of Mabvuku? The boys and girls at Central Forensics Laboratory examined it and concluded that this was the body of a female who died when she was between twenty and twenty-five years old. She had never given birth or had a pregnancy, and she had once suffered from malnutrition as a child. They found out all sorts of trivia about her life! Their hearts must be bursting with pride for having done such a good job uncovering so much about the corpse. They definitely put their backs into it. When you read the file, you'd think the stiff came alive and told them these things. They are certain the cause of death was strangulation (her killer used her own hair extensions). They found the extensions wrapped around her throat and the cervical vertebrae fractured. The body was found in a clearing, near what used to be a council beerhall. About a decade ago, this clearing had a reputation for violent robbery, with gangs waylaying their victims as they went home from a drink or picking up prostitutes. Today, the clearing faces a school, and new houses are being built on it. The boys and girls at Central Forensics say the body was in the ground for no more than fifteen years. There is a ream of paper that explains in jargon why the body was not so badly decomposed, but let's leave those aside for now.

Since there are no reports of a missing person from around the time she disappeared that matches her description, we think this is the body of someone from out of town. Most likely, no one in the area knew she was missing. How could she go missing, if there was no one looking for her?

By the way, did you know that I am now working with Muramba in Missing Persons at the Charge Office?

My probing has revealed that there was one young woman, a prostitute, whose body was also found in that clearing, in 1997. Same as this one discovered this year, no one knew who she was, so she may have been from out of town too. This means our killer, we now think it's the same person, targeted females with no ties to Chizhanje, girls no one would raise the hue and cry over if they did not come home at night. I actually think we should dig up the whole clearing, but I doubt the developers would be particularly pleased about that. Rumours that a piece of land earmarked for development is a mass grave tend to adversely impact property prices.

Yesterday, I got a visit from Timothy Chikomwe of the Central Forensics Laboratory. He showed me the report his team has put together so far. They were lucky to find some papers with the body in a plastic envelope. Moisture had seeped in, naturally, but some of them were still legible. Of particular interest are:

1. A ZUPCO bus ticket for a trip between the City Centre and Mabvuku dated 30 May 1996. (This was found between the pages of the May 1996 edition of *Horizon*).

2. A photograph with the date 17 February 1994, which seems to depict a young woman who might be the deceased or a close friend or relative.

3. There was also some writing in ink. Most of it is faded, but a small part of it is still legible and it reads, "...uilina Chiwande." The photography studio's stamp was also still visible, identifying it as Hassan Studios, with its address in Chegutu.

4. A leaflet inviting people to a church called Pastor Sanyangore Ministries. This church used to congregate in Mabvuku, but it closed down in 1996 after Sanyangore was the subject of an adultery scandal. I know this because my mother's brother was the husband of the woman Sanyangore was caught with.

Chikomwe rang the police in Chegutu. He was told there was a girl called Aquilina Chiwande, who was reported missing in January of 1994. She had been staying with her older sister, Mrs Susan Mhlanga, but there was a falling out between the siblings after Mr Mhlanga began to get friendly towards Aquilina in a rather inappropriate manner. Mrs Mhlanga says she at first thought Aquilina was messing about with her husband, but over time, she started to suspect that her husband was in fact grooming her younger sister, and that he had already molested or tried to molest several of her young female relatives. Aquilina ran away from her sister's home, but did not go back to their parents' home, as the whole family believed what they had been told about her by her older sister. At present, Mr Mhlanga is in jail at Chikurubi Maximum for sexually assaulting his sister's daughter.

So, there it is, Father of Cindy. Maforimbo was telling the truth! Well, partly anyway. There really was a girl called Aquilina.

I had a friend at Mabvuku go through dockets of girls about that age charged with soliciting for prostitution between 1994 and 1997, and he found three of them still living in the Chizhanje area. Two are now married, but the third is still engaged in prostitution. Coincidentally, one of these ladies is called Aquilina, but she is Aquilina Ngwarati. None of them knew of an Aquilina Chiwande. I showed them the picture, and they all said that it has been a while, it was unreasonable to expect them to remember every girl they came across during that period.

This friend of mine also found a man, a Kennedy Ruomba, who used to play with a band at the council beerhall. Ruomba recognised the girl in the picture as one Aquilina, but he did not know her last name. He remembered her by the clothes she wore in the picture. Apparently, Aquilina had slept with his band leader, Never Ndlovu, some time in 1994. Ruomba recalls that Aquilina never returned to the beerhall again. He showed me a picture of the whole band, Madhaka Movement, (ever heard of them? Apparently, they had a song which went *Mangwana mangwana zendemu!* which had some success), taken the evening she ended up at Never's house. There is a girl with the musicians, you can see the top part of her face down to her nose. Ruomba is adamant this is Aquilina. The picture was taken on the 22nd of October 1994.

Most of the band have since died. Of those remaining, one now lives in South Africa and another in Botswana, while yet another is in Mutare. I managed to get hold of the South Africa based one on the phone, a Pikai Zinzou. He told me something shocking. He told me he suspects Never Ndlovu killed Aquilina! and possibly five other girls who frequented the beerhall. His reason is, he claims he found Aquilina's scrunchie, which she had used to tie her hair extensions, in Ndlovu's room two days after he last saw her. Zinzou remembers seeing it on Aquiina when he had run into her at the shops and she had told him she was looking forward to seeing them perform that evening.

Not wishing to get involved, Zinzou ran away to South Africa, and started a new life. He says he knew Ndlovu from childhood, and they were from the same village in Masvingo. Ndlovu was reputed in the community to be unstable. It is possible he knows what happened to the two girls who went missing in the village.

As I type this, there is a man serving a sentence at Chikurubi, charged with the disappearance of one of those girls. He always maintained he was innocent, but the court found him guilty. So, I have initiated the process of reopening the investigation into all the cases where Ndlovu might have been involved.

If Maforimbo says he met Aquilina in 1997, where was she between that year and 1994? Perhaps, she was living as a prostitute in other parts of Harare. It is not easy to get an answer to this one. Police in Chegutu are satisfied that from 1994, Aquilina Chiwande was a missing person under the Missing Persons Act. But the evidence shows me that Maforimbo met Aquilina in 1997. It is also showing me this Aquilina had been dead for two or three years when they met!

I don't know what all this means. You're the one studying Forensics over there in England. If you are coming down to see us this year, perhaps you might help me probe further. I have heard Sambiri of Chitungwiza speak of a Rastafarian team of private investigators there. According to those who know them, they are master sleuths. Talk to him and see if he can get them to look into this matter. We can pool together our money to meet their fee; I cannot let this case go until I get the answer to the questions that are haunting me.

At the same time, I really think perhaps this case requires experts from outside the police profession. I am thinking of those who are said to be able to *see*, if you know what I mean. Don't laugh, boss, I hear that even over there, such things do occur!

THE END

ABOUT THE AUTHOR

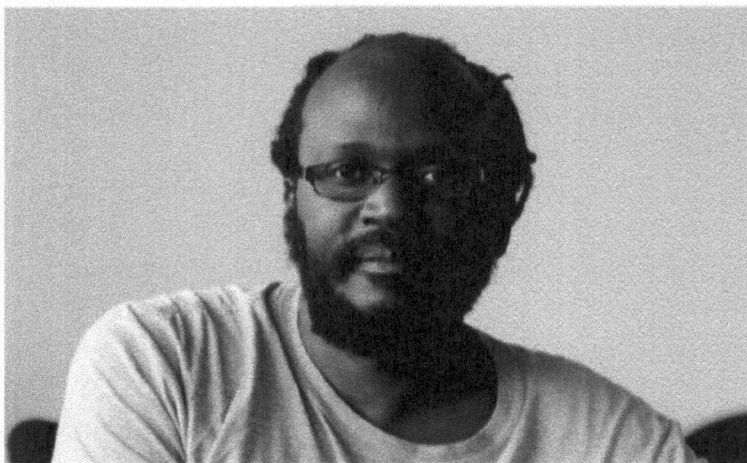

"Impeccably rooted in African mythology with that particular brand of Musodza magic, artfully blending mystical and modern worlds," **Ivor W. Hartmann**, *StoryTime Magazine*, 2008

"If there is one thing that anyone who has read Musodza's previous novel in Shona will have learnt to expect, it is a fearsome monster. He holds up his imaginary monster like a mirror against the real monsters of [Zimbabwean] society"- **Ednah Masanga**, *Amplifying Women's Voices*, 2015

Julius Masimba Musodza was born in Harare, Zimbabwe (then Salisbury, Rhodesia) in 1976, the eldest of five children. He was educated at Avondale Primary School, Harare and St Mary Magdalene's High School, Nyanga before enrolling at the Vision Valley Film, Video & Television Institute in Harare. In 2002, he moved to the United Kingdom.

Musodza's short fiction has been published in anthologies and periodicals around the world and online, such as *AfroSFv3*, *Jungle Jim*, *Omenana*, *Savage Planets*, *Agbowo*, *Lolwe* and others. His *MunaHacha Maive Nei?* is the first definitive science-fiction novel in his native ChiShona language. It was shortlisted in the Book of the Year Category at the Zimbabwe Music & Arts Awards in 2011, which saw him walk away with the Writer of the Year Award. In 2016, *Shavi Rechikadzi* was voted Best Fiction Book of the Year. In the same year, Masimba Musodza was listed among the *10 Best Writers From Zimbabwe* by Culture Trip. He was listed in Geoff Ryman's *100 African Writers Of Speculative Fiction*. He has also written an article for the British Fantasy & Science Fiction Association's *Vector* magazine. He is a member of the Free Speech Union, British Fantasy Society and Don't Divide Us, and has participated in the annual Festival of the Battle For Ideas, which brings together a diverse section of Britain's foremost thinkers and commentators.

Musodza is also involved in the film and TV industry, penning screenplays for independent productions in both England and Zimbabwe, and appearing in background and minor roles in major productions such as *Beowulf: Return To The Shieldlands*, *Vera*, the pilot for the BBC4 show *Make! Craft Britain*, the short film *I Need Help* (Macaw Media Productions, 2018) and TV commercials. He has also performed in local theatre, notably the Arc Performers Group which put on sketch shows at the Arc Theatre in Stockton.

www.masimbamusodza.uk

@musodza

Internet Speculative Fiction Database #230825

9 781914 287855